Nour Alhassan is a management and logistics graduate, with extensive abilities to navigate and handle challenges in various fields such as marketing, journalism, and writing. Her love for writing started in her teenage years. Following her early passion, she worked as a freelance writer at various magazines. Understanding 'Love' and how relationships work is one of her leading passions.

Nour Alhassan

LOVE STORIES SHORT

AUSTIN MACAULEY PUBLISHERS™

LONDON • CAMBRIDGE • NEW YORK • SHARJAH

ISBN – 9789948452959 – (Paperback)
ISBN – 9789948452942 – (E-Book)

Application Number: MC-10-01-2312819
Age Classification: 17+

First Published (2021)
AUSTIN MACAULEY PUBLISHERS FZE
Sharjah Publishing City
P.O Box [519201]
Sharjah, UAE
www.austinmacauley.ae
+971 655 95 202

Preface

It is difficult to understand how relationships work. There is no catalog that comes along with the package called love. Besides, it is so hard to read each other's minds. As a result, some men say that women are difficult to read, and some women proclaim that men don't appreciate or understand them. Therefore, our life together on planet Earth becomes a bit challenging.

Sadly, over the past years the divorce rates jumped up too high and the breakups became uncountable, and all that is happening is not because we can't understand each other but because we can't understand or love ourselves.

Nour Alhassan

Foreword

True love is so rare, do not give up one day and think that you are not lucky enough to find it, because you may be not wise enough to recognize it. Every single person on this universe has a perfect match, a soul mate, a twin flame, whatever you call it. However, you need to dig deep and find them, great things do not come that easy.

I am no expert and I don't have a degree in psychology, thus, this book has nothing to do with the self-help approach; instead you can visualize it as your own personal instruction manual when dealing with relationship's battles.

In this book, I decided to expose some real-life stories that had happened to some couples and present them in a light and breezy way. First, I will briefly explain what had happened to each couple and how everything went south. Next, I will attach a little insight at the end of each story explaining why all those struggles had occurred and how the couple could have avoided them in the first place.

I hope you will enjoy reading this book as I made it as short and straightforward as possible. And put in mind, we are all capable of love and we all deserve to have a loving partner; the only thing that we should do is to take care when we choose our life's companions and make sure that we love them before promising anything.

Love is a promise, so never break it.

Story One

I Do Not Deserve You

Selim is a successful thirty-five-year-old Instagram influencer who devoted all his energy and time to his followers and the agencies he works with.

Three years earlier, Selim was in a terrible position; he was not able to find work, all his jobs were temporary, and he never had an actual job with stable responsibilities and support.

This young gentleman was so desperate, but still, he was certain that everything would turn out just right, and his world will change for the better.

Selim was so good in photography. He worked with some advertising agencies and magazines, but companies always eliminated him for budget cuts.

One day, he decided that he had had enough of all that nonsense, and he opted to start up something by himself. At that time, Selim didn't have the budget to start a business, so he decided to make an account on Instagram and publish his work.

The Instagram account was going well, he got twenty followers in the first two hours, which was not much but it was a good start. The interactions were not a lot either, but Selim didn't give up and kept on publishing his work along with putting as many hashtags as he could stomach. Fortunately, with the help of his family and friends, his account began to grow—he got about two hundred followers in one week.

After five weeks, Selim received a private message on his account from a leading advertising agency asking if he could work for them, as they were in love with his photography and wished to hire him full-time. Without a question, that job offer was an excellent opportunity for him; however, he turned them down because he did not want to work for someone that might fire him anytime. He had already committed with himself that he would build up something on his own. Everyone thought that he was crazy to turn down such an offer, except his parents; they were proud of him and were sure that he was onto something and that he made the right choice.

Long story short, Selim's account began to grow more and more until it hit 250,000 followers in two months. Selim then started to publish sponsored posts for famous brands from all over the world. In such a short time, Selim became a verified influencer on Instagram, and he was always busy with the events and conferences that he got invited to. This young man did it; he followed his dream, and he accomplished his goal.

After one year, Selim began getting paid by Instagram for every picture he published as he hit the 1,000,000 followers, and that was in addition to the commissions he got from the companies he marketed for.

Not so long after his big break, his parents began to be concerned about his love life. Without a doubt, he had become a successful businessman then and all, but they wanted him to start a family too; they did not want him to be overwhelmed by his business and forget about building up a household of his own. Thus, at every family dinner, his parents always brought that subject up, and his friends were concerned too.

One day, Selim's best friend, Ammar, called him and arranged for them to meet for dinner at his house because they hadn't seen each other for a long time. However, the thing that Selim did not know was that the dinner invite was not ordinary; Ammar was trying to hook him up with someone, but, of course, he didn't tell him.

The next day, Selim went to his friend's house.

"Dude, so long. We miss you," Ammar's wife said.

"I miss you guys, too," Selim said. "Where are the little munchkins?"

Ammar then told him that they were at their grandparents' for the day, so they had all the house for themselves for some time. Shortly after Selim's arrival, the doorbell rang.

It was Farida, a drop-dead diva, on the door. She worked as a model in one of the leading advertising agencies and she was also Ammar's wife's friend.

"Hi, Farida, let me introduce you to my friend," Ammar smirked. "This is Selim."

And then Farida and Selim shook hands and took their seats on the dining table.

As a photographer, Selim was mesmerized by Farida's beauty.

Ammar then began to talk about Selim's work and how he was super successful at his business, all to make Farida take notice of him. Ammar was evil when it came to Cupid's works.

The couple chose her because they believed that both Farida and Selim had almost the same interests, and she was a good and respectful woman, and the same went for Selim too.

Not so long after, the dinner ended and everyone was about to go home.

"All that? It is too long for me," Farida fumed while speaking on the phone.

"What's wrong?" Selim asked.

Farida then told him that the Uber driver told her that it would take him one hour to come and she had to go home at that time. And as a gentleman, Selim offered Farida a ride home if she didn't want to wait. However, Farida was shy at the beginning, but that was the only option she had.

She thanked Selim a lot and they went out together.

Ammar and his wife were over the moon, but Ammar didn't look that surprised at the correlation that had just occurred.

"Oh, what a coincidence," Ammar's wife said.

"Yeah, right, a coincidence, alright," Ammar laughed.

His wife then asked him what was going on and she found out that her Cupid husband had arranged everything from the beginning. He told her that he knew Farida did have the Internet on her phone and that whenever she had come to their house before, she had asked for the Wi-Fi password to connect her phone to the network. So immediately Ammar went and turned off the router and that made Farida ask him to book an Uber for her, and sneaky as he was, he did not book the driver. Still, he asked him to stall her and instead agreed to pay him for the ride anyway.

Ten days had passed and Selim was still busy with his business. Genuinely, he had no time for anything else. Even back when he gave Farida, that beautiful lady, a ride, it didn't make much difference—they didn't even exchange phone numbers or interact since.

Ammar was getting so anxious to ask Selim about what had happened with him during the last ten days. Of course, he wanted to know if Selim and Farida had anything special by then. However, he didn't want to ask him directly as for his plan to work.

Selim had an office downtown where he and his crew ran his influencing and promoting business, so Ammar decided to visit him there and find out what had happened so far with his devious yet romantic plan.

"Good morning, dude," Ammar greeted Selim by storming in his office.

"Wow, slow down. Good morning," Selim hissed.

Ammar saw Selim so busy and overflowed with something on his computer; he was speaking with him and his eyes were on the computer.

"What are you doing? Nice ladies there," Ammar smirked.

Selim then told him that he was working on a promotion for a new apparel brand that had nothing to do with the ladies. Ammar didn't know where to start and how to open the conversation about Farida.

"Oh, by the way, thanks for driving our friend Farida," Ammar smiled. "It was nice of you."

Selim then told him that it was his pleasure, and any gentleman in his place would have done that anyway, so there was no need for the thanking.

Mr. Cupid there had realized that to Selim, Farida was not anything special yet. However, he chose to blow his cover and speak directly to Selim.

"Farida is a nice woman. I wish that you could try to know her better," Ammar babbled.

"I smell you in what had happened then with the Uber driver," Selim hinted.

Ammar had then explained to Selim that he needed to give himself a chance and had to try to commit to someone, as no one was getting younger. However, Selim was not very happy with what Ammar was saying, but it made sense. As a result, Selim told him that he would do that, one, for him and he would try to get to know her, she already seemed like a nice person. After a long conversation between Ammar and Selim,

Selim decided to take Farida's phone number and promised to give her a call.

By the time Ammar left, the hesitant man didn't know what to do, and how to start up a conversation with Farida. He then decided to make it a matter of work; he needed a model to make some promotion for a jewelry brand anyway, so Selim thought that he would give her a call and ask her if she would be interested in doing that. And by that, he would not be misleading anyone and would also get his annoying friend out of his way.

Selim then grabbed his phone and called Farida.

"Good Morning, Farida is with me?" Selim asked.

"Speaking. What can I do you for?" Farida responded.

Selim then told her who he was, and from her voice she seemed sincerely pleased to hear from him; she was not annoyed or anything. Afterward, Selim told her that he had taken her number from Ammar because he had a job opportunity for her, and if she was up to it, they could meet at his office and discuss it.

Without hesitation, Farida agreed to meet within three hours. She was such a nice woman, and, also, was excited to hear about that task that she would do. She already had known that Selim was a famous promoter and influencer and that job could help her with her career anyway. On the other hand, Selim had needed a beautiful face to market for that brand, and he had found Farida an excellent fit for that position, not more than that.

The hours had passed, and it was almost time for Farida and Selim to meet.

Farida had arrived on time as usual; she was extremely professional when it came to her work.

They both exchanged greetings and took their seats on the conference table.

Selim began to explain to Farida what he wanted her to do and how much she would earn from that task.

Farida paused for a while thinking about the orientation Selim had made for her, as it was not bad at all and the money was good too.

"Perfect, let me think, and I will tell you my decision today," Farida said.

Selim then thanked her for her time and she left.

At night, Farida called Selim and told him that she had arranged her schedule and that she accepted his offer and asked him when they could start. Thereupon, Selim was thrilled not because he wanted to date her, but because she was a great fit for that job.

Not so long after that, Selim and Farida began to work on the task; a lot of photoshoots and videography were done. They spent more than fifteen hours together for a week. They worked, talked, ate, and laughed.

Both of them had found each other remarkable in a professional and a non-professional way.

And after they finished the promotion, their friendship began to grow and they started meeting a lot. Farida even had a family dinner with Selim's brother and parents once, and she became terrific friends with them too. Of course, his parents and friends thought that she might be the one for him and were so happy for him.

After two months of talking and meeting and Selim's parents' unstoppable requests to be a committed guy, he gave up and decided to take their relationship to the next level. However, he was not feeling anything for her. He respected her and loved her as a friend, but he had said to himself that maybe it was his destiny to not fall in love with his partner at first and it might come later. Besides, Farida felt the same way too. She liked Selim as a friend, not more than that.

One day, Selim was trying to be extra sweet with Farida and sent her a lovely message on her phone with a sweet poem to let her start her morning with. He was typing and erasing, copying stuff from the Internet, and cutting it; honestly, he couldn't find the words. Therefore, he had decided to go to his love Guru, Haitham, his brother, and ask him for help.

Haitham was such a romantic and he had always known what to say and when to say it, especially when it came to love.

Haitham was happy to help his brother out. He took his phone and started writing.

"Good morning, I hope you will have a great day today. Wake up and let the sun shine over the universe. The people are waiting for your bright light," Haitham typed.

Selim found that breathtaking and thanked his brother. After five minutes, Farida had replied with a beautiful picture of a sun and some kind words. However, the poor man didn't know how to answer. So, he ran to his brother once again for the help.

Many days had passed like that; Selim or technically Haitham and Farida were exchanging messages and love letters nonstop. Farida was so surprised; she didn't think that Selim could write that. She fell in love with all the words. Yet, she was concerned because when she and Selim met, he seemed to be a completely different person. Honestly, she liked him better when they texted.

Farida became so attached to her phone. Every morning, she waited on fire to receive the lovely message that brightened up her every morning.

On the other hand, Haitham too was always looking forward to Farida's astonishing replies. Surprisingly, Haitham began to feel something weird toward that girl, and it showed whenever he met with her. When he caught a glimpse of her talking or smiling, he was over the moon. He didn't know what he was feeling, but clearly, he was blocking everything in and establishing himself in balance; at the end that was his brother's girl and he would never do that to him. However, sometimes he felt that Selim was not in love or even cared for Farida, and it was so impersonal of him to let his brother send the messages. Moreover, Selim even didn't bother to check Farida's replies.

One day Haitham decided to talk to Selim about the whole thing, because it was not very noble to keep on deceiving Farida like that and it was time they stopped.

Haitham went to Selim at his office and opened up about all that. Selim also told him that he was feeling guilty and they needed to end that, and also that he should tell Farida about everything and let her choose either to forgive him or not.

While they were both talking, Farida texted Selim with a fantastic poem.

Selim then put down his phone and looked at his brother.

"Well, just that one time," Selim begged.

Haitham took a long breath and accepted.

"Okay, that will be the last time," Haitham responded.

Unfortunately, what Selim and his brother didn't know was that Farida was outside Selim's office door waiting for him to text her back, so she could surprise him and enter with beautiful flowers that she made for him.

When Haitham texted her, Farida immediately entered the room to find Haitham holding Selim's phone and typing with her chat window on.

"What is that?" Farida growled.

"I can explain. I didn't mean to," Selim apologized.

Suddenly Haitham stood up and apologized to Farida and left. Farida was furious. However, after Selim told her about the whole thing, she stormed out of his office after throwing the flowers in his face.

Farida was so hurt and felt humiliated. She couldn't understand how something like that could happen to her. It was all a lie, a filthy disgusting lie. On the other hand, Selim didn't know what to do as he was a villain in that scenario.

Selim tried for several days to apologize to Farida, but she was not returning any of his calls or texts. As a result, he gave up and tried to forget about the whole thing. Alternatively, Haitham was feeling so bad not only because he was the deceiver but because he hurt Farida, the last thing that he could ever think of. He knew that what he did was wrong, but he got attached to her to the extent that he couldn't stop himself from being with her even if it was just by texting.

After one month, Haitham went to his brother and asked him about Farida. However, his brother's answer was not very pleasant; he told him that she cut herself out and told him that she never wanted to speak with him or his brother again.

"Do you love her?" Haitham asked.

"No, Haitham," Selim replied. "I was trying to, but I couldn't."

Haitham was so sad to hear that Farida was feeling that way, and he was sure that she was hurting. After a long time of thinking, Haitham decided to go to Farida and tried to explain to her why that had happened and make her forgive him.

By that time, Farida was shooting an ice cream commercial in Gouna, a resort in Hurghada city, and Haitham found out from her Instagram posts that she was there then. As a result, he decided to go and meet her in person.

After a six-hour drive from Cairo to Hurghada, Haitham had been reciting what he would tell her. No words in the universe would have been enough apology for what he had done. He was so down and miserable.

Eventually, when Haitham arrived in Gouna, he put his bags at the hotel and went to the place that Farida was shooting her commercial at.

He saw Farida from a distance, sitting on a lazy boy by the sea, waiting for the director to ask them to resume shooting. Without hesitation, he went straight to her.

"Farida," Haitham mumbled.

Once Farida saw Haitham's face, she was about to storm out, but he quickly grabbed her hands and told her that he drove all that distance to apologize to her.

"Your brother didn't have the guts to do it himself, so he sent his wingman," Farida scoffed.

Haitham had then explained to her that that had nothing to do with his brother though. He had come there to apologize for himself and not on behalf of anyone whatsoever.

"I know what we did was bad," Haitham said, "and you have all the right to be angry."

"Yes, of course, I know that. But how could you do that?" Farida said.

The poor man explained to her that texting her was the only thing that made him happy throughout his day, and that whenever he saw her, he could not stop himself from admiring every aspect of her personality. Texting her was like a drug to him, he couldn't stop. He had been living in a parallel universe and was daydreaming that all her replies were meant for him and not his brother.

Farida was surprised at what Haitham told her. She took a deep breath and told Haitham that she used to be so confused about her almost relationship with his brother and that she was not attracted to him at all when they would meet in person, but when she was away from him and the texts started to pop, she always felt something different. And at that time she found out why.

After a long talk, Farida accepted Haitham's apology and forgave him, and he told her that that was the only thing that he needed to hear from her.

"Maybe if you came clean with me, there might have been a chance to know you better," Farida said. "But both of you made it so awkward for anything to happen."

Insights

Never force love, on someone or yourself. Love should come to you organically. However, you should open your heart, of course, first and believe in it. But believe it or not, sometimes the people around us affect our decisions. It would help if you didn't give your ears to anything you do not wish to do in the meantime. And that is what happened in that story.

Selim was guilty and a victim too. He was blameworthy because that was not a genuine way to treat Farida. He was deceiving her without a care in the world. Also, Selim couldn't love Farida; he was forcing himself to have feelings for her to please his parents and friends, and that is not what love is about. Love comes on its own without any brown nosing or interference from anyone.

On the other hand, what had happened to Haitham was not pleasant either. He fell for Farida and, technically, Farida did fall for him too.

To elaborate, Farida was not attracted to Selim but to the texts that were sent by his brother.

Haitham and Farida could have had a beautiful life together, but after the betrayal and the fact that he was Selim's brother, it was not very appropriate for them to be together.

To summarize, do not force yourself to love someone, because that will bring the devil in you and make you do stuff that you will not be proud of or want to do from the beginning. Let love come to you; the only thing that you can do is to open your heart and be ready to receive love.

Story Two

If It's Meant to Be, It Will Be

It was a peaceful morning. Everything was great. The sun was shining so bright, and the air was so breezy and warm.

Meet Liam, an eighteen-year-old college student. He is so smart and extremely handsome.

This young man was the definition of a perfect man; he was so amazing with his family and friends and helpful to others.

Meantime, it was the summer vacation, and Liam was searching for a job to keep him busy and bring him extra cash and experience. Sadly, he didn't find any job, so he decided to put all his energy in sports.

Liam put on his tracksuit and trainers and went for a jog. After some time, his phone rang, it was his best friend, Serena.

"Hey, dude," Serena said. "Movies after two hours?"

It was quite early for a movie, but Liam didn't mind and told her that he was in.

Serena, how to describe that girl? She has such a remarkable personality; she is like the female version of Liam. However, they have some differences, of course, but they are alike in almost everything, even in the annoying stuff, LOL.

"Call zee and the rest and let them join us," Liam told Serena.

After an hour of jogging, Liam went home to get ready for the movies. He took a shower, drank his protein shake, and headed out to pick up Serena and go to the mall.

Of course, it was taking forever for Serena to come down.

And finally, Serena showed up after fifteen minutes of waiting.

"Seriously. All that time," Liam frowned at Serena.

"Look who is talking," Serena responded.

"The movie will start, and everyone is waiting for us," Liam said.

Serena then told him that she was sorry. She was trying to pick her outfit, and, of course, that was a reasonable reply, because Serena was a little OCD when it came to her looks.

Serena and Liam reached the movie theatre on time; they didn't miss anything. They saw their friends there waiting for them by the door so they could all enter together.

The movie was about a romantic story between two people in a long distance relationship. During the movie, Serena mocked Liam about how a particular couple in the movie remind her of him and his girlfriend.

"Oh, that is you and Renata," Serena laughed.

"Zip it and watch," Liam responded.

Renata, Liam's girlfriend, was a sweet but controlling person. She lived in Paris which was so far away from where Liam was. However, they both tried their best to make their relationship work. They both had been dating since high school. After high school Renata left for Paris to study at Sorbonne.

Serena always mocked Liam about his relationship because she knew that he was not in love with Renata and he was just with her because he was trying to keep his promise to her, not more than that. And that was right. Liam was uncomfortable with that relationship and deep inside he wanted to end it. Suddenly, Liam's phone had started ringing, and everyone was shushing him at the movie theatre. It was Renata.

Liam stood up to go out and answer the phone.

They both talked for ten minutes. Renata was checking on him and telling him about her day. However, Liam was not talking much because he was a bit annoyed; the man was out with his friends and watching a movie. Honestly, Renata was kind of not caring a lot about Liam's circumstances. He told her that he was out with his friends and they were watching a movie. Hence, she should have hung up and called him later; instead, she kept on talking without a care in the world.

When they were ending the call, Renata asked Liam who he was with. Liam then named everyone at the outing. It was a bit interfering on her part, but Liam didn't mind.

"Serena again," Renata hummed.

"What do you mean?" Liam responded.

Renata then said that he hung out with Serena almost every day and every night and that she was not comfortable with that.

As a matter of fact, they both had a bit of a fight, as Liam told her that she was his best friend since high school, and he would not limit his relationship with her because she was not comfortable with that. As a result, Liam excused himself from the call and told Renata that he needed to go back inside to his friends because it was so rude to leave them all that time.

Liam was angry and frustrated by that call, but it was the usual thing between them, their calls always ended with a fight.

When Liam went back inside and took his seat, Serena felt that he was not okay, but she chose not to bring up the subject.

Instead, she tried to cheer him up by doing some silly faces while offering him some of her popcorn.

Both Liam and Serena were not watching the movie; Liam was on his phone resuming his fight with Renata on WhatsApp, and Serena was also on her phone trying to find silly jokes and send them to Liam to distract him and let him end that obvious fight with Renata.

After some time, the movie ended and everyone left. Meanwhile, Liam and Serena chose to go for some lunch at the mall.

Liam could not take it anymore and chose to open up to Serena about the fight he had had with his girlfriend.

"Renata is unbelievable," Liam said. "I am this close to ending it."

"It's okay, calm down," Serena soothed. "What happened?"

Liam then told her that Renata had no respect for what he was doing. Everything had to be according to her schedule only, and also, he added that she was jealous of her because they were out and about 24/7.

"Wait, what?" Serena giggled.

Serena told Liam that maybe she was just insecure because they were far from each other. However, Liam didn't think that that was a good excuse for her. He never did that to her. Liam was not jealous of any of her guy friends and he trusted her. He thought that she was so childish and still had that high school attitude.

Serena didn't know what to tell Liam, because Renata was clearly not sensible at all.

Thereafter, the waiter came and took their order, and, of course, they had ordered the same healthy plate: Avocado toast with chicken breast and sunflower seeds. That was their signature plate since high school.

"See, we too still have that high school mentality," Serena gushed. "Same plate for three years."

Liam then had a great laugh after the joke that Serena cracked. That girl always knew how to make him smile and feel better; she was a keeper.

"You know how to make me smile," Liam sighed at Serena. "Thanks for being in my life."

"Am always here, bro, not going anywhere," Serena declared.

A sound from behind them said, "May I take a minute of your time?"

Liam and Serena turned and looked to find a pretty woman with a folder in her hand. They asked her to have a seat.

The lady then introduced herself; her name was Sharon and she was the PR Manager of an event organizing company that was hosting a massive event in the city called the City Champions Race. It was like the Formula One event.

"Honored. How can we help you?" Liam asked.

Sharon then asked Serena and Liam if they were interested in working at that event because she thought that their posture and looks fit. She gave them her business card and asked them if they could come for the walk-in-interview along with their CV the next day at four o'clock in the Millennium hotel.

However, they both were surprised by the speedy job offer, but they accepted and assured her that they would come.

"Perfect, and if you have any friends that want to join, just refer them to me," she said. "And you will make extra money with every eligible person you will bring in."

After Sharon left, Serena told Liam that that was a great opportunity, as that event was so popular and would be a massive add-on to their resume. Liam agreed and said it was also an excellent chance to kill time and earn some extra cash.

Afterwards, Serena and Liam left the mall with a beautiful meal in their stomach and a great job offer.

Unfortunately, the roads were packed up, it took Liam and Serena forever to pass for the main road, but it was fun. They always had a great time together. Liam also opened up to Serena about his feelings toward Renata. And that he could not do that anymore, not because of the long distance but because of Renata's childish way and her poor understanding.

Serena didn't want to meddle in his relationship; she didn't want to make him do something that he might regret, but at the same time, she didn't want him to be in a relationship that was not right for him. However, Serena chose to zip her mouth and mind her own business.

A day had passed, and it was time for Serena and Liam to go to the interview. They did refer some of their friends to Sharon via her email.

The organizing company that Liam and Serena were about to work for was one of the leading companies in the region. They hosted the walk-in interviews in a five star hotel and booked a fancy ballroom too.

Liam went to pick up Serena, as usual, that day and also picked up the rest of his friends. Liam loved carpooling.

Finally, Liam and his friends reached the hotel and went directly to the place they were directed to by the front desk.

The ballroom was so luxurious; there was a vast open buffet breakfast for the potential candidates to eat in before they started the interview.

Every candidate was greeted with an attractive colorful binder that had everything about the event the company was arranging. Everything was well organized and perfect.

After they all had breakfast, it was time for them to begin the interview.

Sharon Spotted Serena and went directly to her.

"Oh, Serena, good morning, guys," Sharon smiled. "I am so glad you got all the folks. Let us start with you guys."

The ballroom was so busy with college and high school students, and it was so great of Sharon to pick them first.

Sharon started the interview with Serena, followed by Liam, and then the others. Everyone was so kind and had a lot of skills that mesmerized Sharon, especially Liam, as he had worked in many events since high school. Hence, the interview was a success for all. Every single one was assigned a job that was most suitable for their skills and experiences.

First, Liam was going to be responsible for the fan zone booths, and Serena was going to be responsible for the merchandising. Everyone else was assigned different jobs like salespeople and cashiers at the fan zone.

Eventually, after the interview ended, Sharon and the crew thanked everyone for coming and wished the best for those who were not eligible for the job.

The event was going to start the next day at 7 a.m., and as a result, Serena and Liam decided to go home and prepare themselves for that time.

Liam was so excited and couldn't wait to start. Also, he wanted to get his mind off Renata's shenanigans and to get busy with something else. On the other hand, Serena was also eager to start her job. She loved merchandising and was so happy that she was going to spend that time with her beloved best friend.

At 6 p.m., Liam was about to go to sleep as he had to wake up early the next day. As he was getting ready to sleep, his phone rang, and, of course, it was Renata.

"Hello," Liam gasped.

"Hey babe, what is wrong with your voice?" Renata asked.

Liam then told her that he was about to sleep to wake up early for work.

Renata was surprised as Liam hadn't mentioned anything about the new job to her.

"Renata, we just fought," Liam bellowed.

"Yes, but update me, at least," Renata shouted.

The poor man was so annoyed and told her that it was not very classy of her to start a fight with him and expect that everything would be normal afterward and that she hadn't even apologized about her behavior.

"Okay, I am sorry for snapping the other day," Renata said. "I just miss you."

Later, both of them patched up. And Liam told her all about what had happened on that day and how the interview went.

"You and Serena again? Even in a summer job," Renata snapped.

"What is your problem with Serena?" Liam responded.

Renata told Liam that it is too much on her. He was spending all his time with Serena. Furthermore, she felt uncomfortable with that.

After a long talk of trying to tell Renata that it was his best friend and that was not something new to her; however, the three of them used to always hang out together since high school. Though, the only thing that had changed was that Renata moved away. Renata then told him that she was not very happy with that relationship, and she asked him to choose whether he would hang out with Serena or wanted to be with her. Thus, and without thinking, Liam told her that he chose Serena, and he was sick and tired of the child-like behavior. Besides, Liam didn't like to be on the spot like that. As a result, Liam broke up with Renata and thanked her for that call that ruined his quiet night before work.

A new chapter in Liam's life was about to begin. Finally, he dared to confront Renata with all the things he felt about her, and how she had been ruining everything beautiful in their relationship. However, it was hard on him, but he was strong enough to spill the beans at last.

Liam didn't feel sad at all; he thought that he broke free. He had been dating Renata for five years: the first three years were perfect, but everything went south when Renata changed and became so jealous and unreasonable. Though Liam was still keeping his promise to her to be together forever no matter what. But he had had enough with all the things that she was doing.

Liam woke up that day with a smile on his face and an urge to start that fresh day with no dramas and no girlfriend.

Meanwhile, Serena got up and was preparing herself to go to work. She was so excited and had too much energy for that day. While Serena was having breakfast, her phone buzzed to find a message from Renata. The message was so mean and dull.

"Good Morning, S. Hope you are happy now. Liam and I broke up because of you, I always knew that he was in love with you, but the thing that I can't understand is how you could do this to me. We used to be best friends. I wish you a happy life with your new boyfriend."

Serena was so surprised and annoyed by that. All the energy she had just went away and converted into anger and rage for Renata. Nevertheless, Serena chose not to reply and decided to speak with Liam first.

Afterward, Liam called Serena asking her if she needed a ride, but she told him that her dad would drop her on his way as the venue was too close to his work. Her voice was very shaky and confused and that made Liam concerned about her.

"Are you okay?" Liam asked.

"Yes, I'm fine, I'll tell you when I see you," Serena responded.

At 6.30 a.m., everyone arrived at the meeting point, waiting for the Quay Circuit to open (the place that was hosting the event).

Liam and Serena decided to have breakfast at a nearby coffeehouse before they went to work. Liam was waiting at the coffee house for Serena.

By the time Liam ordered coffee, Serena had arrived. She looked so cloudy and had puffy eyes; she never knew how to hide her feelings.

"Wow, what is the matter with you?" Liam asked.

Without hesitation and before even saying good morning to him, Serena showed him the message she had received from his ex, Liam was full of rage and anger.

"What the hell! I will call her and show her now who she is dealing with," Liam snapped.

"Liam, why is she saying that? I didn't do anything to you guys," Serena cried.

Liam explained to Serena what Renata had been feeling about her. And he didn't want to tell Serena because he didn't want her to think that he wanted to limit his relationship with her.

And told her that Renata put him on the spot and told him that he needed to choose whether to cut her off of his life or stay with Serena, and that's why they had broken up.

Serena was so surprised. She looked at Liam with grateful eyes and couldn't believe what he had done.

"You chose our friendship over her?" Serena soothed.

"Of course, you mean more to me than her," Liam responded. "And that is what made me realize that I am not in love with her anymore."

Serena was concerned that Liam did that out of rage. Yes, she was happy to know that she meant a lot to him, but at the same time she didn't want him to regret what he did.

She placed her hand on his shoulder and said, "Liam, you could have put that conversation on hold until you both cooled it down."

After Liam took a sip of his coffee, he paused for quite long and, he told Serena that he had been trying to find a way out to escape that relationship, and that was it.

Serena was relieved to see that Liam was pleased about his choice, and that she had nothing to do with his breakup.

From a distance, Liam could see that the Quay opened, and everyone was getting inside.

"Let us go to them. It is almost time," Liam said to Serena.

When they reached the quay, they found Sharon waiting to welcome all the employees and make a quick orientation about the nature of the work.

After that, Liam went to the fan zone to check whether everything was all right and in place while Serena was checking the promotions and flyers that would be passed on to the guests, and how every shop was presented.

That day was a success; all the employees were doing pretty well, and Liam was killing it. He was such a fantastic organizer and audit.

While everyone was busy working, Liam thought that he should go and check on Serena and see if everything was alright. At that time, Serena was helping a fellow employee with her cashier responsibility as the girl didn't know how to swipe a credit card for a guest. So, Serena deliberated to help her out and show her how to do the swipe right and also as to which copy she had put at the cash register and which one she gave to the customer. Liam was standing there admiring Serena's hard work. Serena was so busy that she didn't even see him standing there. However, something weird had happened. When Serena gave the customer his copy, Liam found that the man was beginning to chat with her, and he gave her his business card.

This customer was so handsome and looked important. He looked like those people who worked for Apple and Microsoft.

Liam was worried if that man was bothering her, so he stepped forward to the customer with a power pause and asked him if everything was all right.

"By the way, sir, it is not appropriate to pass your business card to employees," Liam rebuked.

The customer looked at him in a strange way and said, "And you are?"

"I am the one who is responsible for the fan zone," Liam responded.

The customer then apologized and whispered at Liam's ear and said, "I think that she doesn't mind that anyway."

Liam was raging and was about to get in a fight with him, but Serena grabbed him from his hands immediately and took him far from the booth.

"Liam, you could have made a scene," Serena said.

"I wish, he is a perv," Liam shouted.

"It is okay. I took care of it," Serena responded. "I even slashed his card in front of him and threw it."

Liam then told Serena to take care of herself and buzz him if she was bothered by anyone else. Serena told Liam that she didn't need a bodyguard and that she could take care of herself; however, it felt nice when he told her that. She was so grateful.

Liam then left with a huge question mark on his face. He was so surprised and asked himself why he had overreacted like that? Did he get jealous, or he was just overprotective because she was his best friend.

"This is Serena," he gushed.

She was like a sister to him. Or Renata's words were getting to him.

Liam then put everything on the side and resumed working.

On the other side, Serena's tasks were making her busier and busier. She was sitting on her desk trying to print more flyers and brochures for customers.

"Hey, sorry to intrude, your name is Serena, right?" an employee asked Serena.

"Yes," Serena smiled.

"You are lucky to have a boyfriend like that," the employee said to Serena.

Serena looked at her with a wide-opened eyes and said, "He is not my boyfriend, but he is my best friend."

The employee rolled her eyes, and then she apologized for the misunderstanding.

For that moment, Serena was so confused; she felt kind of shy and happy when that girl thought that Liam was her boyfriend. However, she didn't dwell on that thought and continued working on her tasks.

The day was over and the event was a success. Everyone was waiting at the meeting point for Sharon to sign them off and give them their paychecks for the day.

Serena was trying to avoid Liam, she didn't know why. On the other hand, Liam was trying to bypass Serena too. It was so weird, maybe something had happened there. While Serena was walking, she found Liam at her face.

"Well, here you are," Liam said.

Serena then smiled and told him that she had fun, and it was a great experience.

They both sat by the bench in silence.

Not so long after that, Sharon had arrived at the meeting point, and she thanked everyone and gave the paychecks out, and all the employees left.

In the meantime, Liam, Serena, and their friends were in Liam's car. Everyone thanked both of them so much for recommending them and to give them that great work opportunity.

So many days had passed and the awkwardness that was between Liam and Serena was fading away, as a result of what had happened at the work event. Serena and Liam's relationship began to take a different road; something was different. There was so much fondness, warmth, and affection. They even began to call each other by their pet names. They began talking for hours on the phone and shared every little thing. One day Liam video-called Serena while she was having breakfast because he didn't see her that day and was missing her face.

Five months had passed on that rhythm.

Liam and Serena's feelings for each other had begun to grow and take a different direction; both were surprised.

Serena didn't know what was happening to her, but she felt that she could be falling in love with her best friend. Still,

Serena was scared that she could become a rebound buddy for Liam as that had happened right after he broke up with Renata. For that reason, she chose not to open up about her feelings to him or anyone. Serena said to herself that maybe he was just becoming extra sweet with her because his mind was clear now as he had got rid of that toxic relationship he was in.

On the other hand, Liam was sure that he was falling for Serena, and that was not something strange or brand new because he used to like her before too, but he didn't have the chance to tell her that because she was dating someone else by that time.

Summer was over and the university had started. Every one of Liam and Serena's friends were noticing how both were getting closer. It was apparent to all that their relationship was more than being just best friends.

The University Student Union always welcomed back the students with a free buffet breakfast at the cafeteria. Since Serena was the president of the SU, everything was compelling, the ambiance was amazing, and everyone was enjoying their time.

"Thanks, S., the food is amazing," Leona smiled.

Leona was one of Serena's colleagues; she was a lovely young woman.

After a while, Liam entered the cafeteria and greeted his friends.

"You are a real Boss," Liam said to Serena.

"Thanks, babe," Serena laughed.

After the feast came to an end, everyone went to their lectures full and happy.

Serena and Liam were at the same college and classes, except for the chemistry elective.

It was chemistry class for Serena, she put on her gown and glasses, and the professor began to teach.

"Welcome all. I hope you had a great summer," Professor Rashid said.

Mohanad Rashid was the head of the Science Department, and not anyone could take his class. He was sweet but tight when it came to grading. However, Professor Rashid was different from the other professors. He was young and very helpful to his students. All his students loved him.

Professor Rashid then assigned the lab partners and gave the students a brief about what they were going to cover throughout the semester.

Unfortunately, Serena was assigned to an annoying lab partner; his name was Nader.

Nader was so obsessive-compulsive, exactly like Mr. Monk Series or maybe more.

The poor young woman was so disappointed with Mr. Neat and know-it-all by her side, but what could she do, she had to keep up with him for the coming three months of her life.

On the other side of the campus, Liam was attending his Graphic design class, that class was impressive. The students made designs of their own on their computers and then use sublimated papers and printed it on any apparel they chose, and the best thing there were NO LAB PARTNERS.

Finally, when the day was over and classes ended, Liam texted Serena and told her to meet him at the football field.

Serena then went there to find Liam waiting for her with a huge smile on his face; it was as if he wanted to tell her something.

"Oh, hello," Liam murmured as Serena was coming. "Does this remind you of anything?"

Serena then took a deep breath as if she was recounting the good times.

"Yes, our high school football field," Serena responded.

Liam then told Serena that she was the most beautiful girl at high school and that he wished that that beautiful girl would be his girlfriend, but she was dating someone else.

Serena stared surprisingly at Liam and said, "What? You're kidding, right?" and looked the other way; she was kind of shy.

"No, I am not," Liam smiled.

There was a moment of silence there, as Serena was trying to catch her breath from that brand-new information.

Serena then grabbed Liam's hands and asked him, "Are you high?"

Without hesitation Liam looked into her eyes and told her that he was always high whenever she was by his side.

Serena was melting after that look Liam gave her; she was this close to telling him how she felt about him. It was such a romantic moment that they both experienced, until Nader's interruption.

"Hey, S., I have been looking all over the campus for you. Let's go work on the project now," Nader said.

"Nader," Serena rebuked, "the deadline is after one month."

"Yes, I know, so we better start now," Nader insisted.

Liam then told Nader that they were in the middle of a conversation, and it was rude of him to interfere like that.

However, Serena told Nader that they could work on this project next week, and if he did not like that, he could talk to Professor Rashid and ask him to change his lab partner.

Sadly, the moment was over, Nader just ruined it, and it was almost time for Serena to head home.

On Serena's way home, she was thinking about what Liam had said. She asked herself what he had meant by that? Was he trying to tell her something, or was it just a memory he liked to share with her? At the same time, Liam thought that Serena was not getting his hints and that she was not into him and would never be.

Three months had passed, and nothing new had happened between Liam and Serena. It seemed like they were in love, but they were not dating. It was almost time for the winter break, and Serena's family was planning to go to New York for the holidays.

On the last day of university before the spring break, Serena told Liam that she wanted to speak with him before they flew to New York.

Consequently, after they had finished their last lecture, they went for a walk at the park, and Serena began to speak.

"Liam, what is all that?" Serena said.

Liam was confused by the question and asked her what she meant by it. She then elaborated more and told him about how their relationship was taking a different direction. Serena added that she felt something for him, but she couldn't say it because she didn't know what he felt and that she didn't want to ruin their relationship because of a misunderstanding. However, she took a leap of faith and spilled the beans.

"I think I am in love with you," Serena said.

It was a shock to Liam, and he didn't think that Serena would reciprocate to what he felt deep inside his heart toward her. Liam didn't tell Serena about his feelings from the beginning because he loved her so much that he thought that she might deserve better than him. Though, that was wrong because you never choose for someone.

After what Serena said, Liam paused for a while, and quickly held Serena's hands and told her that he loved her too. From the moment he laid eyes on her, he was trying to get her to notice his love, but then he thought that she maybe deserved someone better than him and that is why he chose not to say anything to her.

Serena was angry at Liam for saying that.

"What are you saying?" Serena gushed. "You have always been the one."

Insights

In that story, Liam and Serena were experiencing what we call a twin flame connection.

People always confuse a twin flame with a soul mate. Those are entirely different connections. A soul mate is a person that fits perfectly in your life, they are the people whom you will always go to for advice, and if you need a cheer up moment, you just run to them to boost your confidence. In short, they are your soul's companions. They can be your friends, family members, a passersby or "the cat down the road" quoted by Ralph Smart.

Not anyone can be your twin flame, it takes only a special someone (opposite gender) to be your twin.

The moment you meet your twin flame is the moment the earth will stop moving from under your feet. A twin flame is a spiritual connection that awakens you and makes you feel things you have never felt before in your life; it's like hitting a high level of glee. You are each other's mirror; you can both see through each other (freaky ha!!!). Also, you will have no filters or egos with your twin flame, and all your retouches will fade away the moment you speak to them. At the beginning of the connection, you might experience some weird sensations, like sleepless nights as you can't get them out of your head, your appetite may get so high or so low. This connection might feel strange and may overwhelm you because all those things happened in the blink of an eye. It's like you have just clicked without forcing any emotions or not being yourself for one second.

Your twin flame is always there in your life with or without your observations. Both of your experiences have been in sync from the moment you were born. Besides, you should have crossed paths before; you could have been friends, colleagues, or even just two strangers who shared a settee in an airport or a club, but still, you must have met at least once. However, some people are just lucky enough to reunite with each other so early, and others don't, for it was not their time to hitch. Yet, their souls unquestionably have recognized each other, but their hearts were in preparation mode. As result, all the relationships they might have before connecting with their twin flame will end. They will never continue their lives with someone who are not their twin flame that they have once recognized.

Some people think that they might have been cursed in love or something as all their relationship fall apart. Though, everything happens for a reason and God tries to put them on the right path toward their twin flame. You always need to think positive even if the situation is so hard on you.

To summarize, Liam and Serena were destined for each other. Nevertheless, it was not their time to reunite when they first met, because to be reunited with your twin flame and start your relationship with them, you need to be whole and updated. A twin flame will come into your life not to complete

you but to form with you a divine force of love.

Story Three

Love Is a Choice

Wedding bells were ringing; everyone was waiting for the bride to come. The aisle was filled with wondrous white lilies and pink confetti. It was Sara and Mazen's wedding. A lovely couple that loved each other dearly.

Mazen and Sara had met last summer at Sharm el sheik. They dated for twelve months and decided to get married the next year, when they both realized that they were madly and truly in love with each other.

Meanwhile, it was time for Sara to show up with her dad. Mazen was so amazed by that beautiful girl walking toward him, the steps she was taking seemed to take so long, he wanted her to run to him, he couldn't wait to tell her his vows, and kiss her.

When Sara's dad was about to give his only daughter to her soon-to-be-husband, he had a short conversation with him.

"Mazen, I am giving you a piece of my heart," Akram said.

"Not to worry, Uncle, she is my life," Mazen smiled as he took Sara's hands.

Akram, Sara's dad, Mazen, Sara, two of their relatives, and the Sheikh had their seats on the table placed at the front of the ballroom, and they started to exchange the vows. Then the Sheikh began to cite the responsibilities and rights of the marriage contract.

Not so long after the Sheikh's speech, Sara and Mazen signed the marriage agreement and they were officially married.

"Congratulations, you guys," the Sheikh said. "May you have a wonderful life together."

Mazen then gave Sara a long sincere hug that made their eyes water. It was like, finally, we got married and will be together forever.

The applause was so loud, and the Zagharid were nonstop. Zagharid is a folkloric tradition done in the Middle East as a way of showing their happiness at weddings or any happy events. It is like whistling sounds.

Sara's Mother, Amany, was so happy to see her daughter a happy bride. She couldn't feel more pleased to see that her little girl became a beautiful bride. Also, Mazen's parents were over the moon that their young man finally found his bride that loved him dearly.

Sara and Mazen chose to make the wedding ceremony small and short; the couple wanted to save the money for a big honeymoon trip to Europe.

Everyone then went to the cruise dinner to have the wedding in. It was a restaurant cruise in the Nile. The ambiance was terrific, Mazen booked a large table there that accommodated his guests. And as a wedding surprise for the happy couple, the restaurant management decided to book the whole restaurant for them exclusively and free of charge for them to have an extra special celebration and not be bothered by strangers. It was lovely of them. Egypt is always known for its genuine hospitality and marvelous etiquette.

Eventually, Sara and Mazen took their seats. And after a while, Rahaf and Fadi showed up and took their places too beside the bride and groom.

Rahaf and Fadi were the couple's best friends. Mazen and Sara always admired them too. They are the definition of love and sacrifice; they had been married for ten years with no complications and had two amazing kids.

"Congratulations, I'm so happy for you guys. Finally," Rahaf grinned.

"Thank you," Mazen smiled back.

Everyone was busy dancing to the music and celebrating that special day with the newlyweds.

After long hours of dancing, singing, laughing, and eating, the wedding celebration ended, and the newlyweds went to their honeymoon suite at the airport hotel as they were traveling to Paris to start their honeymoon trip the day after.

When they arrived at the hotel room, they were amazed by the setting. The room was spotless, and the roses were covering the floors, not to mention that giant heart of lilies that was on the bed. Sara gazed at Mazen and said, "This is the best day ever."

Mazen was so pleased that Sara was that happy. He then told Sara that he would do all he could to make her happy, and he would never let her shed a tear. Sara was delighted to hear that; she wrapped her arms around him and assured him that he would be the happiest husband in the whole universe.

The next morning Sara and Mazen woke up with a massive smile on their faces. It was such a grace to find themselves next to each other on the same bed. It felt heaven-like.

Thereafter, they finished packing their bags and went down to the checkout desk to find both of their parents and siblings waiting by the lobby to escort them to the airport and wish them a blissful honeymoon.

That made them so happy and surprised.

"Congratulations, my darlings," Amy (Mazen's mother) said.

"Thank you, Aunt Amy," Sara said.

Amy then told her that from that moment onward she would call her mom.

"Is it okay, Amany?" Amy smiled to Amany.

"Of course, Ames, she is your daughter too," Amany approved.

Finally, all the bags were placed at the trolley, and they had reached the airport.

After everyone said their goodbyes, Sara and Mazen went inside and headed to the check-in desk.

"Congratulations. I believe that you are our newlyweds," the check-in desk employee congratulated them.

And then she made an upgrade for them to first class.

"Oh, thank you so much," Sara and Mazen babbled at the same time.

"It is nothing, hope you enjoy your honeymoon," the lady responded.

After they had finished the check-in procedures, Sara and Mazen went to the first-class lounge to wait for their plane and have some snacks. While they were sitting on the table, Sara paused for a while and had a long look at her husband's eyes. She remembered the first moment when they had met, and the first fight they had had and how, for the past year, they overcame every conflict and bad things that had happened between them. She was so proud. Sara and Mazen were always a happy couple. Still, at the beginning of their relationship, they had a lot of misunderstands and struggles that might have led them to break up. Again, they never did, and they chose to resolve anything that came their way because they had chosen to love each other forever.

Meantime, positive energy was flying among them; everything was going smooth for them since the wedding. All the things they had saved for and didn't do, just came their way: a private wedding, first-class tickets, and a wonderful honeymoon suite. It was meant to be, and it was as if the universe was showering them with gifts.

After a four-hour flight, Sara and Mazen had arrived in Paris, the city of romance. They didn't have many bags, just two handbags and two other personal items. That made it easier for them to get out of the airport fast. They just spent an hour finishing all the processes needed to enter the country.

Mazen had pre-booked a car to drive them to the hotel from the airport, to avoid delays and crowd. He wanted Sara to be comforted and calmed.

When they arrived at the pick-up gate, they found a man holding a banner with their names. It was Pierre, their driver.

Mazen and Sara then went to him and told him that it was them that he was expecting.

"Bonjour, sir, madame," Pierre acknowledged.

He took their bags and escorted them to the car.

"Where are we headed, sir?" Pierre asked while driving out of the airport premises.

"To the Lovers Nest Hotel in Port Mailout," Mazen responded.

Mazen and Sara booked a room in a charming boutique hotel in a neighborhood called Porte Mailout, and it was walking distance to the Champs Elysees and all the attractions there. Besides, it was a romantic hotel.

Finally, they had arrived at the hotel, the ride took about an hour and a half from the airport, and it was a busy morning. The hotel was so cozy, and it was like staying at your grandmother's house. The restaurant was so warm and felt like home. Even the food there looked homemade and delicious, that was the real Paris.

After the couple entered that lovely hotel, Mrs. Leona, the Hotel Manager, gave them a warm welcome and escorted them to their room.

Mazen and Sara were so mesmerized by the room's interior design and that fantastic small balcony overlooking Eifel Tower.

After they settled in, they went to explore the city. By that time, Sara was very hungry, so they decided to go for lunch at the Champs Elysees. After a long time trying to pick a restaurant, they finally decided to go to a healthy restaurant they had found. Both Sara and Mazen were so robust when it came to eating; they always picked healthy choices.

Sara picked the lentil pasta dish with chicken, and Mazen chose to have the avocado toast dish with tuna.

Immediately, and after they finished their lunch, they went back to the hotel to have some rest to recharge themselves as they wanted to be wild and go clubbing at night.

Lastly, it was midnight, Sara and Mazen started to get ready for the night and went to the club.

The club was also at a walking distance from the hotel. It was so good and the music were amazing. They danced like no tomorrow; the couple was going on nonstop; it was so refreshing and crazy that it made them so tired and so sleepy.

The next day, Mazen woke up before Sara, and he decided to get her breakfast in bed as a romantic gesture.

After so long, Sara woke up to find a beautifully handsome man standing in front of her with a rose in his mouth and holding a huge tray that had all the best breakfast choices that she liked. It was Mazen, of course,

"Gosh, that face in the morning is just everything," Sara smiled and took the tray from his hand and gave Mazen a colossal kiss and warm hug.

After they filled their tummies with that amazing Parisian breakfast, Sara and Mazen decided to go to Eifel Tower and take some pictures and send to their friends and family as a way to share that fantastic moment with them.

The weather was remarkable and the atmosphere was to die for. They took a lot of pictures and videos.

The people Sara shared those pictures with were, of course, her parents and her friend Rahaf. However, it took

Rahaf hours to reply, and it was not like her at all and that made Sara so worried about her. After some time, while Mazen and Sara were having coffee at a coffeehouse near the Eifel tower, Sara called Rahaf to check on her. But when Rahaf answered, her voice was not so good.

"Honey, are you okay? Sick?" Sara said.

"No, Sue, I am okay. Just tired a bit," Rahaf responded with a groaned voice.

Sara didn't buy it anyway, and she chose to wait until she went back to Cairo and see what had been going on with her.

By that time, Fadi was on the phone with Mazen to check upon him, and his voice was not that good too.

After Sara's phone call with Rahaf had ended, she put down her phone and looked at Mazen.

"Babe, I think there is something wrong with Rahaf," Sara said.

"I think Fadi too," Mazen rejoined.

However, they both chose to put that thought on hold and enjoy their honeymoon and not spoil their moods with anything at that time.

In the afternoon, Sara suggested that they go by the Seine river. She heard that there were a lot of fun things to do and a lot of artists that can draw a portrait of them. Not to mention the countless gift shops. Mazen loved the idea and they both went there.

One day was left for Sara and Mazen to leave Paris and head to the rest of the countries they had planned to visit in Europe. As a result, they decided to go to the Louver museum and rest for the day.

Mazen's plan was to visit the rest of the countries by the Eurostar train, and it was a good idea. They visited so many countries; they went to Spain, Italy, and Amsterdam. It was the best trip ever. Besides, the train journey alone was a breathtaking experience.

Sadly, their Euro honeymoon was about to end, and they were heading home the next day.

"I can't believe I will be going to work tomorrow," Sara grumbled. "But I miss my folks."

"I know, but it is good to be back to our home, baby," Mazen smiled.

Sara assured him that she is more than happy that they will be under one roof, finally, and that she couldn't wait to share her life with him as a lovely married couple.

Sara and Mazen were finally home; it was so strange and unusual for them to be alone in their apartment for the first time. Sara felt joy and happiness.

"It was not a dream," Sara babbled. "We are married."

Mazen was filled with joy to see Sara so happy like that, and he told Sara that he, of course, loved his parents' house and it once was his house too, but this felt different. Mazen felt home, and with her by his side, it felt like a kingdom to him.

"I love you, Sara, so much," Mazen smiled and kissed Sara's hands.

After they unpacked, Mazen suggested that they go to the supermarket and get groceries and other stuff.

"Okay, dear, let me check what we need. I'll go to the kitchen," Sara said.

When Sara went to the kitchen, she opened the fridge to see what they had to get. Surprisingly, she found that the refrigerator was packed with stuff (cheese, cold cuts, water, fruits, vegetables), and the freezer also had different types of beef, chicken, and fish.

"Oh my god. Who did that?" Sara rejoiced.

Mazen heard Sara's loud voice. He thought something had happened to her, so he ran to the kitchen and found that everything they needed was there, even the spices and the oils were in the kitchen cupboards.

"I am sure our parents did that," Mazen smiled.

Immediately Sara called her mother and asked her if she knew anything about what had happened in their kitchen.

"Yes, Sue. Me, your dad, and Mazen's parents did that. I hope you liked it, darlings," Amany giggled.

Sara and Mazen were so happy with their parents' kind gesture, they were so tired anyway to go to the supermarket and shop, and that did rescue them, especially when they had to wake up early in the morning and go to work.

After they had a quick dinner, it was time for them to go to sleep, but then Sara remembered that she needed to call Rahaf and tell her that they had come back. Also, she was worried about her since Paris and wanted to check up on her.

Sara then grabbed her phone and dialed Rahaf's number.

"Weird! Rahaf's phone is off," Sara said to Mazen.

"Let me call Fadi," Mazen responded.

Instantly, Mazen called Fadi and told him that they had come back and that Sara was trying to call Rahaf, but her phone was off. By that time Sara was standing beside him, so eager to know what was wrong; she was anxious. However, after Mazen asked Fadi about Rahaf, his face became so sad as if he was about to break the phone off.

"Are you serious? Okay, we will talk at work tomorrow," Mazen said to Fadi. "Good night."

Sara was so scared of what Mazen was about to tell her, but she could not wait to find out.

Mazen then looked at Sara with disappointed eyes and said, "Rahaf and Fadi got a divorce."

"What? How?" Sara fumed.

Sara was so frustrated and surprised as to how come they got a divorce after ten years of a fairytale marriage, plus they seemed fine at the wedding.

Meantime, Sara and Mazen had quite a shock, but they had nothing in their hands to do at that time, so they decided to sleep on it until the next day.

The next morning Sara and Mazen got up, had breakfast, and got ready to go to work.

Mazen was the marketing manager at an advertising company, while Sara was deputy editor-in-chief of one of the leading magazines in Egypt.

By the time Sara reached the magazine, her phone was ringing. It was Rahaf. Without hesitation, Sara went back inside her car as she was about to enter the building, and she answered.

"Rahaf, I know about the divorce," Sara agonized. "Are you okay?"

"When I see you, we will talk." Rahaf responded. "Let's meet for coffee during your break."

They both decided to meet after two hours at a coffeehouse near Sara's work in Zamalek and talked about what had happened between Rahaf and Fadi that led to a divorce.

Not so long after Sara's call with Rahaf, Mazen met Fadi at work, and they spoke about the whole thing at Mazen's office.

"Mazen, it was not meant to be," Fadi said. "We just realized that all the feelings were just gone."

Mazen was raging at that moment, he hit the desk with his hands and told Fadi that they just realized that after ten years and two kids.

"Are you out of your mind?" Mazen snapped.

Fadi then calmed him down and told him that that was not only his decision and that Rahaf was on the same page with him too.

However, Mazen had a lot of work, so they could not finish talking. As a result, Fadi suggested that they could resume the talk at lunch, and he went to his office.

A couple of hours had passed, and it was time for Sara and Rahaf to meet at the coffeehouse.

Rahaf was there when Sara arrived. When Rahaf saw Sara coming, she stood up and ran to her, giving her a big hug and wailing in her embrace.

"Rahaf, why are you crying?" Sara sighed.

"Nothing, I just missed you so much." Rahaf sniffled.

Sara didn't buy it, and then they took their seats. After a long pause of staring, sniffing, and crying, Sara asked Rahaf to tell her what happened and how all that occurred in a blink of an eye. Therefore, Rahaf started to say the whole story to her. She told Sara that all the conflicts began in the past three years. They were always fighting about silly things and one day she found out that Fadi was cheating on her with another woman and that was it for her. Though, later Fadi apologized and promised her that he would never do that again and she forgave him and forgot about the whole thing. Still, after that incident their relationship was fragile, and a hole was formed in their bond. They began to resent each other, and, in a blink of an eye, all their feelings for each other were utterly gone, and they wanted a divorce.

Consequently, Sara was mute, and she did not know what to say. How the fantastic couple that was madly in love could end up like that. They were so meant to be; they loved each other the moment their eyes met; they even got married after two months of dating, and their marriage lasted for more than ten years. Sara was sorrowful and disappointed.

Sara then looked at Rahaf and said, "But you could have chosen to wait and fix your marriage. That was a rushed decision."

Sara then told Rahaf Just as she and Mazen have had lots of fights and arguments when they were dating, but that made their relationship much stronger because when you solve the conflict, there comes the understanding and fixing.

"I am sad, Sara, but I am over it," Rahaf responded. "The kids are my concern now."

And she added that she just didn't want them to feel anything and tried to make their lives as normal as it could be.

Afterward, Sara's break was about to end, so she wished that Rahaf made the right choice and told her that they should finish their conversation later after her work.

Meantime, Sara went back to work with a huge question mark on her face. She was so annoyed to find that Rahaf got over the love of her life that quickly; she always got to know when Rahaf hid her feelings, but this was different. Rahaf was telling the truth; she was entirely over Fadi. And Fadi felt the same way too, and it was so obvious when he was talking to Mazen about it. It seemed that both of them got over each other so quickly, was that love? Do not think so.

Insights

Love is a choice not a feeling. It is not a term to be defined, not even an emotion someone can express, it differs from one person to another; though some common conditions are the same to all.

Feelings come and go. You cannot be happy, sad, amused, or down all the time. But only if you choose to.

True love is trust, respect, patience, forgiveness, courage, appreciation, sacrifice, and so much other stuff, and you can keep counting. It also has a spiritual side that no one can genuinely outline, and that is the first spark that you once felt. However, some people define this spark as an 1ation: an intense, short-lived passion. But still, it is the first stage of falling in love.

In my opinion, a woman could never genuinely forgive her partner if he cheated on her, even if she forgave him, deep inside she would always remember what he has done. On the other hand, if a man cheats and is immediately forgiven, that will not make him feel loved; no, that will actually make him subconsciously disregard and disrespect his partner more and more in the future. However, when we compromise our dignity for love, then this is not love. And vice versa if the woman was the cheater.

To sum up, in that story, Sara and Mazen chose to love each other; they spent a year before they decided to get married, not because they were not in love with each other, but because it is not that easy to choose to love someone. It takes time and effort to work on the relationship first. In contrast, Fadi and Rahaf's relationship was so hasty. They didn't choose to love each other. They just let their feelings sway them. As a result, when they began having some severe conflicts, the feelings were going away, and their love for each other was fading until it was completely gone.

Sometimes, we fall in love because we are lonely. As a result, we think passively; we need the person but not want them. We just need to feel loved by someone, and this is by far the most selfish thing anyone can do. Love is selflessness, it is when you give all you have to make your significant other happy and comfortable without caring about their state. To elaborate, you can't just fall out of love with someone because they are in a bad mood or act weird. That is why love is a choice, not a feeling.

Think of it this way.

If your partner, one day, was experiencing some hard issues and became very defensive, arrogant, and in the worst mood. As a matter of fact, if love was a feeling, you will ignore them and treat them the same way, especially if you asked them what is going on with them, and if they didn't give you an answer. On the other hand, and to prove my point that love is a choice, if you chose to love that person, you would want to sacrifice for them, their lousy behavior and temper will not affect your love to them, but it will make you feel concerned about them, and you will try to comfort them by any means possible. For instance, you might surprise them with a flower when they feel down, tell them a joke to make them laugh, and so many other things. Thus, you chose to be kind to them; you have worked on your relationship, and you chose to.